The Three Railway Engines

THE REV. W. AWDRY

WITH ILLUSTRATIONS BY
C. REGINALD DALBY

RANDOM HOUSE NEW YORK

Thomas the Tank Engine & Friends

GULLANE

Based on The Railway Series by the Rev. W. Awdry

Copyright © Gullane (Thomas) LLC 2003

All rights reserved under International and Pan-American Copyright Conventions.

Published in the United States by Random House Children's Books,

a division of Random House, Inc., New York, and simultaneously

in Canada by Random House of Canada Limited, Toronto.

Originally published in Great Britain in 1945 as Book 1 in The Railway Series.

First published in this edition in Great Britain in 1998 by Egmont Books Limited.

ISBN: 0-375-82408-1   Library of Congress Control Number: 2002110427

PRINTED IN ITALY   10 9 8 7 6 5 4 3 2 1

www.randomhouse.com/kids

www.thomasthetankengine.com

RANDOM HOUSE and colophon are registered trademarks of Random House, Inc.

DEAR FRIENDS,

When *The Three Railway Engines* was first published in May 1945, a foreword to it was probably not considered. Within six months, however, it became clear that the book wasn't going to be the slight affair that had perhaps been expected. Twenty-five books were to follow, all of them with forewords, in a sequence that became known as *The Railway Series;* and yet, despite numerous reprintings, the little book which started the wheels turning remained without a preface.

Now, for this new edition, more than fifty years later, a foreword is thought appropriate. I feel very privileged, not only to have been asked to write it, but to have the chance to dedicate the book's stories to the memory of my father, their creator.

CHRISTOPHER AWDRY
THE AUTHOR'S SON

Edward's Day Out

Once upon a time there was a little engine called Edward. He lived in a shed with five other engines. They were all bigger than Edward and boasted about it. "The Driver won't choose you again," they said. "He wants big, strong engines like us." Edward had not been out for a long time; he began to feel sad.

Just then the Driver and Fireman
came along to start work.

The Driver looked at
Edward. "Why are you sad?"
he asked. "Would you like
to come out today?"

"Yes, please," said Edward.
So the Fireman lit the fire and
made a nice lot of steam.

Then the Driver pulled the lever, and Edward puffed away.

"*Peep, peep,*" he whistled. "Look at me now."

The others were very cross at being left behind.

Away went Edward to get some coaches.

"Be careful, Edward," said the coaches, "don't bump and bang us like the other engines do." So Edward came up to the coaches very, very gently, and the shunter fastened the coupling.

"Thank you, Edward," said the coaches. "That was kind; we are glad you are taking us today."

Then they went to the station, where the people were waiting.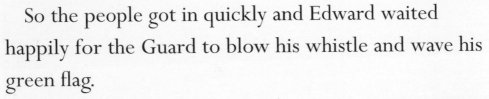

"*Peep, peep,*" whistled Edward – "get in quickly, please."

So the people got in quickly and Edward waited happily for the Guard to blow his whistle and wave his green flag.

He waited and waited – there was no whistle, no green flag. "*Peep, peep, peep, peep* – where is that Guard?" Edward was getting anxious.

The Driver and Fireman asked the Stationmaster, "Have you seen the Guard?" "No," he said. They asked the porter, "Have you seen the Guard?" "Yes – last night," said the porter.

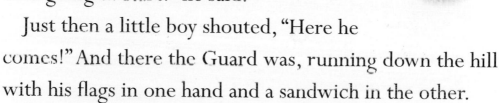

Edward began to get cross. "Are we ever going to start?" he said.

Just then a little boy shouted, "Here he comes!" And there the Guard was, running down the hill with his flags in one hand and a sandwich in the other.

He ran onto the platform, blew his whistle, and jumped into his van.

Edward puffed off. He did have a happy day. All the children ran to wave as he went past, and he met old friends at all the stations. He worked so hard that the Driver promised to take him out again the next day.

"I'm going out again tomorrow," he told the other engines that night in the shed. "What do you think of that?"

But he didn't hear what they thought, for he was so tired and happy that he fell asleep at once.

Edward and Gordon

O ne of the engines in Edward's shed was called Gordon. He was very big and very proud.

"You watch me this afternoon, little Edward," he boasted, "as I rush through with the Express; that will be a splendid sight for you."

Just then his Driver pulled the lever. "Goodbye, little Edward," said Gordon as he puffed away, "look out for me this afternoon!"

Edward went off, too, to do some shunting.

Edward liked shunting. It was fun playing with trucks. He would come up quietly and give them a pull.

"Oh! Oh! Oh! Oh! Oh!" screamed the trucks. "Whatever is happening?"

Then he would stop and the silly trucks would go bump into each other. "Oh! Oh! Oh! Oh!" they cried again.

Edward pushed them until they were running nicely, and when they weren't expecting it, he would stop; one of them would be sure to run onto another line. Edward played till there were no more trucks; then he stopped to rest.

Presently he heard a whistle. Gordon came puffing along, very slowly, and very crossly. Instead of nice shining coaches, he was pulling a lot of very dirty coal trucks.

"A goods train! A goods train! A goods train!" he grumbled. "The shame of it, the shame of it, the shame of it."

He went slowly through, with the trucks clattering and banging behind him.

Edward laughed and went to find some more trucks.

Soon afterwards a porter came and spoke to his Driver. "Gordon can't get up the hill. Will you take Edward and push him, please?"

They found Gordon halfway up the hill and very cross. His Driver and Fireman were talking to him severely. "You are not trying!" they told him.

"I can't do it," said Gordon. "The noisy trucks hold an engine back so. If they were coaches – clean sensible things that come quietly – now that would be different."

Edward's Driver came up. "We've come to push," he said. "No use at all," said Gordon. "You wait and see," said Edward's Driver.

They brought the train back to the bottom of the hill. Edward came up behind the brake van ready to push.

"*Peep, peep, I'm ready,*" said Edward.

"*Poop, poop, no good,*" grumbled Gordon.

The Guard blew his whistle and they pulled and pushed as hard as they could.

"I can't do it, I can't do it, I can't do it," puffed Gordon.

"I will do it, I will do it, I will do it," puffed Edward.

"I can't do it, I will do it, I can't do it, I will do it, I can't do it, I will do it," they puffed together.

Edward pushed and puffed and puffed and pushed as hard as ever he could, and almost before Gordon realized it, he found himself at the top of the hill.

"I've done it! I've done it! I've done it!" he said proudly, and forgot all about Edward pushing behind. He didn't wait to say "Thank you," but ran on so fast that he passed two stations before his Driver could make him stop.

Edward had pushed so hard that when he got to the top, he was out of breath.

Gordon ran on so fast that Edward was left behind.

The Guard waved and waved, but Edward couldn't catch up.

He ran on to the next station, and there the Driver and Fireman said they were very pleased with him.  The Fireman gave him a nice long drink of water, and the Driver said, "I'll get out my paint tomorrow and give you a beautiful new coat of blue with red stripes; then you'll be the smartest engine in the shed."

The Sad Story of Henry

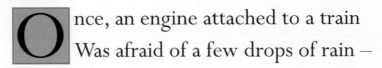

Once, an engine attached to a train
Was afraid of a few drops of rain —

– It went into a tunnel,
And squeaked through its funnel
And never came out again.

The engine's name was Henry. His Driver and Fireman argued with him, but he would not move. "The rain will spoil my lovely green paint and red stripes," he said.

The Guard blew his whistle till he had no more breath, and waved his flags till his arms ached; but Henry still stayed in the tunnel and blew steam at him.

"I am *not* going to spoil my lovely green paint and red stripes for you," he said rudely.

The passengers came and argued too, but Henry would not move.

Sir Topham Hatt, a director who was on the train, told the Guard to get a rope. "We will pull you out," he said. But Henry only blew steam at him and made him wet.

They hooked the rope on and all pulled -- except Sir Topham Hatt. "My doctor has forbidden me to pull," he said.

They pulled and pulled and pulled, but still Henry stayed in the tunnel.

Then they tried pushing from the other end. Sir Topham Hatt said, "One, two, three, push" – but he did not help. "My doctor has forbidden me to push," he said.

They pushed and pushed and pushed, but still Henry stayed in the tunnel.

At last another train came. The Guard waved his red flag and stopped it. The two engine Drivers, the two Firemen, and the two Guards went and argued with Henry. "Look, it has stopped raining," they said. "Yes, but it will begin again soon," said Henry. "And what would become of my green paint with red stripes then?"

So they brought the other engine up, and it pushed and puffed and puffed and pushed as hard as ever it could. But still Henry stayed in the tunnel.

So they gave it up. They told Henry, "We shall leave you there for always and always and always."

They took up the old rails, built a wall in front of him, and cut a new tunnel.

Now Henry can't get out, and he watches the trains rushing through the new tunnel. He is very sad because no one will ever see his lovely green paint with red stripes again.

But I think he deserved it, don't you?

Edward, Gordon, and Henry

E dward and Gordon often went through the tunnel where Henry was shut up.

Edward would say, "*Peep, peep — hullo!*" and Gordon would say, "*Poop, poop, poop! Serves you right!*"

Poor Henry had no steam to answer; his fire had gone out. Soot and dirt from the tunnel roof had spoiled his lovely green paint and red stripes. He was cold and unhappy, and wanted to come out and pull trains too.

Gordon always pulled the Express. He was proud of being the only engine strong enough to do it.

There were many heavy coaches, full of important people like Sir Topham Hatt, who had punished Henry.

Gordon was seeing how fast he could go.

"Hurry! Hurry! Hurry!" he panted.

"Trickety-trock, trickety-trock, trickety-trock," said the coaches.

Gordon could see Henry's tunnel in front.

"In a minute," he thought, "I'll *poop, poop, poop* at Henry and rush through and out into the open again."

Closer and closer he came – he was almost there when crack: *"Wheee ——————— eeshshsh."* He was in a cloud of steam and going slower and slower.

His Driver stopped the train.

"What has happened to me?" asked Gordon. "I feel so weak." "You've burst your safety valve," said the Driver. "You can't pull the train anymore."

"Oh, dear," said Gordon. "We were going so nicely too. . . . Look at Henry laughing at me." Gordon made a face at Henry and blew smoke at him.

Everybody got out and came to see Gordon. "Humph!" said Sir Topham Hatt. "I never liked these big engines — always going wrong; send for another engine at once."

While the Guard went to find one, they uncoupled Gordon and ran him on a siding out of the way.

The only engine left in the shed was Edward.

"I'll come and try," he said.

Gordon saw him coming. "That's no use," he said. "Edward can't pull the train."

Edward puffed and pulled and pulled and puffed, but he couldn't move the heavy coaches.

"I told you so," said Gordon rudely. "Why not let Henry try?"

"Yes," said Sir Topham Hatt, "I will."

"Will you help pull this train, Henry?" he asked.
"Yes," said Henry at once.

So Gordon's Driver and Fireman lit his fire; some
platelayers broke down the wall and put back the rails;
and when he had steam up, Henry puffed out.

He was dirty, his boiler was black,
and he was covered with cobwebs.
"Ooh! I'm so stiff! Ooh! I'm so stiff!"
he groaned.

"You'd better have a run to ease your joints, and find
a turntable," said Sir Topham Hatt kindly.

Henry came back feeling better, and they put him in front.

"*Peep, peep,*" said Edward, "I'm ready."
"*Peep, peep, peep,*" said Henry, "so am I."

"Pull hard, pull hard, pull hard," puffed Edward.

"We'll do it, we'll do it, we'll do it," puffed Henry.

"Pull hard, we'll do it, pull hard, we'll do it, pull hard, we'll do it," they puffed together. The heavy coaches jerked and began to move, slowly at first, then faster and faster.

"We've done it together! We've done it together! We've done it together!" said Edward and Henry.

"You've done it, hurray! You've done it, hurray! You've done it, hurray!" sang the coaches.

All the passengers were excited. Sir Topham Hatt leaned out of the window to wave to Edward and Henry, but the train was going so fast that his hat blew off into a field, where a goat ate it for his lunch.

They never stopped till they came to the big station at the end of the line.

The passengers all got out and said, "Thank you." And Sir Topham Hatt promised Henry a new coat of paint.

"Would you like blue and red?"

"Yes, please," said Henry. "Then I'll be like Edward."

Edward and Henry went home quietly,
and on their way they helped Gordon back
to the shed.

All three engines are now great friends.
Wasn't Henry pleased when he had his new
coat. He is very proud of it, as all good engines
are — and he doesn't mind the rain now.
He knows that the best way to keep his
paint nice is not to run into tunnels but
to ask his Driver to rub him down when
the day's work is over.

OTHER TITLES IN
THE RAILWAY SERIES